Grangeville

by Samuel D. Hunter

SAMUEL FRENCH

FOR PRODUCTION INQUIRIES

UNITED STATES AND CANADA

info@concordtheatricals.com

1-866-979-0447

UNITED KINGDOM AND EUROPE

licensing@concordtheatricals.co.uk

020-7054-7298

Each title is subject to availability from Concord Theatricals Corp., depending upon country of performance. Please be aware that *GRANGEVILLE* may not be licensed by Concord Theatricals Corp. in your territory. Professional and amateur producers should contact the nearest Concord Theatricals Corp. office or licensing partner to verify availability.

No one shall make any changes in this title(s) for the purpose of production. No part of this book may be reproduced, stored in a retrieval system, scanned, uploaded, or transmitted in any form, by any means, now known or yet to be invented, including mechanical, electronic, digital, photocopying, recording, videotaping, or otherwise, without the prior written permission of the publisher. No one shall share this title(s), or any part of this title(s), through any social media or file hosting websites.

For all inquiries regarding motion picture, television, online/digital and other media rights, please contact Concord Theatricals Corp.

MUSIC AND THIRD-PARTY MATERIALS USE NOTE

Licensees are solely responsible for obtaining formal written permission from copyright owners to use copyrighted music and/or other copyrighted third-party materials (e.g. artworks, logos) in the performance of this play and are strongly cautioned to do so. If no such permission is obtained by the licensee, then the licensee must use only original music and materials that the licensee owns and controls. Licensees are solely responsible and liable for clearances of all third-party copyrighted materials, including without limitation music, and shall indemnify the copyright owners of the play(s) and their licensing agent, Concord Theatricals Corp., against any costs, expenses, losses and liabilities arising from the use of such copyrighted third-party materials by licensees. For music, please contact the appropriate music licensing authority in your territory for the rights to any incidental music.

IMPORTANT BILLING AND CREDIT REQUIREMENTS

If you have obtained performance rights to this title, please refer to your licensing agreement for important billing and credit requirements.

GRANGEVILLE was first produced by Signature Theatre (Emily Shooltz, Artistic Director; Timothy J. McClimon, Executive Director) in New York City on February 4th, 2025. The production was directed by Jack Serio, with set design by dots, costume design by Ricky Reynoso, lighting design by Stacey Derosier, sound design by Christopher Darbassie, and casting by Caparelliotis Casting. The dramaturg was John Baker. The cast was as follows:

ARNOLD . . . . Brian J. Smith
JERRY . . . . .Paul Sparks

CHARACTERS

ARNOLD – Male, early forties. Jerry's half brother.
JERRY – Male, early fifties. Arnold's half brother.

SETTING

A void and liminal space.

TIME

The present.

AUTHOR'S NOTES

Shifts forward in time occur whenever the stage direction "transition" appears.

During phone call and video call scenes, phones and computers should not be physically represented.

Dialogue written in *italics* is emphatic, deliberate; dialogue in ALL CAPS is impulsive, explosive. Dialogue in [brackets] is implied, not spoken.

A "/" indicates an overlap in dialogue. Whenever a "/" appears, the following line of dialogue should begin.

Ellipses (…) indicate when a character is trailing off; dashes (–) indicate where a character is being cut off, either by another character or themselves.

(**JERRY** *and* **ARNOLD** *appear.*)

(**JERRY** *waits nervously, taking a deep breath. He makes a call.*)

(**ARNOLD** *considers whether or not to answer. He finally does.*)

ARNOLD. *(Non committal.)* Okay…

(*There is a long silence between the two of them.*)

(*Finally:*)

JERRY. Is it – late over there?

(*Pause.*)

I'm guessing it's gotta be later over there! Yep, you –.

(*Short pause.*)

Anyway hi.

ARNOLD. This bill isn't itemized.

JERRY. Uh – what?

ARNOLD. The bill, the PDF you just emailed me, it doesn't even say what these charges are for –

JERRY. Oh, uh – yeah, it's sorta a mess, Mom isn't good at paying bills as it is, but she wouldn't let me touch any of it, / so –

ARNOLD. Well if I'm going to help you with this I need more information, I need something itemized, or –

JERRY. Oh, yeah, it – I was talking to Candice, you remember Candice!

ARNOLD. No.

JERRY. Sure you do, Candice! Her family had that big house over near the Dairy Queen. I dated her sister when I was in high school for a while! She's dead now actually. Got drunk and drove the wrong way down the Lewiston grade –

ARNOLD. What does this have to do with this bill?

JERRY. Oh! Sorry, she, uh. That's what she does now. She's a – you know, at the hospital. She's works in accounting or whatever. She said she could get everything together for me. It's just a little complicated with the paperwork, power of attorney –

ARNOLD. Just – send me her contact info, what's her name –

JERRY. Candice! You remember Candy Apple!

ARNOLD. Send me her contact info and I'll do it myself. Something is obviously going on with Medicaid, I'm sure Mom just messed something up with the paperwork, / she –

JERRY. Arnie. Hi, Arnie.

(Pause.)

It's good to hear your voice.

(Pause.)

ARNOLD. Let's *please* not make this more complicated than it needs to be. I don't know why we have to do this over the phone –

JERRY. Oh you know, I'm terrible at email, if we could just talk it through –.

ARNOLD. Seriously, I can take care of all of this, just send me what's-her-name's info from the hospital / and –

JERRY. I can't say hi to you? We can't just say hi?

(Pause.)

ARNOLD. Hi, Jerry.

(Pause.)

Now let's just try to focus on / this –

JERRY. Stacey told me she might wanna split up.

*(Pause. **ARNOLD** lets out a breath.)*

ARNOLD. Shit.

(Pause.)

I'm sorry.

JERRY. Thanks.

(Pause.)

I mean it's not a done deal, I think there's a good chance we can make it, but. She wanted me to move out, so. I moved out.

(Pause.)

ARNOLD. Are the kids taking it okay?

JERRY. Yeah, they're okay. Lauren's in college now, she's busy doing her own thing. I think she saw it coming anyway. Tom took it harder than I thought he would, but –. He'll be okay.

ARNOLD. Was there...? I mean did one of you...?

JERRY. Nah, no cheating, we're not that interesting.

ARNOLD. So what happened?

JERRY. I think Stacey just – realized she wasn't happy.

(*Short pause.*)

ARNOLD. What about you?

JERRY. Oh I've never been happy. Heh.

(*Short pause.*)

God knows what I'm gonna do if she leaves me. We've been together since I was nineteen! What am I gonna do, download one of those apps?!

ARNOLD. Uh-huh.

JERRY. You'll have to show me how to use it!

(*Pause.*)

ARNOLD. What?

JERRY. Oh, I just... I figure you know that stuff better than me.

ARNOLD. I've been with Bram for seventeen years, why would I know –?

JERRY. Oh, I just thought... I mean I thought gay guys...

(*Pause.*)

Shit, I'm –...

(**JERRY** *trails off.* **ARNOLD** *seethes.*)

ARNOLD. Anyway, have you talked with anyone from Medicaid? What did they say *specifically*?

JERRY. Well I don't know.

ARNOLD. What do you mean?

JERRY. Mom wouldn't tell me. She just kept saying that she'd take care of it herself. You know her. Like I said in the email, it wasn't until I got this bill from the hospital that I realized, they're barely covering any / of the –

ARNOLD. Well can you ask Mom, then?

(Short pause.)

JERRY. Oh, uh –. Arnie, she's not – talking anymore.

(Silence.)

ARNOLD. Oh.

(Pause.)

How – long has she –?

JERRY. Ever since that second stroke, it's –...

(Pause.)

I mean you can still talk *to* her, the doctors say she might still understand. Who knows, maybe hearing your voice after all this time will snap her outta it! Like that movie, you know, with the guy from *Goodfellas*? He's in a coma and then the *Jumanji* guy / gives him –

ARNOLD. What the hell are you talking about?

JERRY. I really don't know, I'm sorry.

(Pause.)

ARNOLD. Look, just –. Do you have her Medicaid card?

JERRY. That I have.

ARNOLD. Okay, just – take a photo of it and text it to me. Worst-case scenario, do you think she has enough money in the bank to cover this bill?

JERRY. Eesh... I don't know... Hopefully?

ARNOLD. I assume she doesn't have any investments, or anything like that –

JERRY. *(Chuckling.)* Not unless you count the sculpture.

(Pause.)

ARNOLD. Sculpture? What sculpture?

JERRY. You know, that sculpture she found in that pawnshop out in Burley from a few years back. You know.

ARNOLD. No...

JERRY. She never mentioned it to you?!

ARNOLD. I haven't talked to her in a while.

JERRY. But I mean this was *years* ago! You hadn't talked to her in that long?

ARNOLD. No. I mean she –. She left me a voicemail a few months ago. I never responded.

(Short pause.)

JERRY. Oh. Well anyway, she was convinced she found a long-lost piece of art by that famous artist – Jack something? Anyway, it's this sculpture of a real tall skinny guy, all stretched out. Famous sculptor. Jack something.

(Short pause.)

ARNOLD. Wait – are you talking about Giacometti?

JERRY. That's it. She was convinced that she found a long-lost Giacometti at this pawn shop in Burley.

(Pause.)

ARNOLD. Okay, I – don't know what to do with that, but in any case, she doesn't have any *real* investments, right?

JERRY. Nah.

ARNOLD. Is there anything in the trailer worth selling?

JERRY. C'mon, she's not dead / yet –

ARNOLD. I just don't want to wait to have this conversation, okay? I think I remember there being some kind of silver set from her mom? Is that right?

JERRY. She gave that to Mark Chillis. Couple years back.

ARNOLD. Why?

JERRY. He got married. To that biker chick, what's her name, you remember her. Face tattoos.

(**ARNOLD** *lets out a rueful laugh.*)

ARNOLD. Figures.

JERRY. What?

ARNOLD. Nothing.

JERRY. I mean I could – try to get it back?

ARNOLD. It's not about the silver, it's…

(Pause.)

When Bram and I got married, she –. She didn't even call.

(Pause.)

JERRY. Yeah, I –. I know, Arnie.

(Silence.)

(Then, suddenly:) She really doesn't have a problem with you, Arnie.

ARNOLD. Okay, we are not doing / this –

JERRY. I'm just saying, I want you to know that. She doesn't have a problem with you being [gay] –, you know. I know that for sure. I think it was just, you got married over there in Amsterdam and Mom's never even been to the East Coast let alone Europe, and she was just kinda confused about the whole thing and she didn't know if you even *wanted* to hear from / her –

ARNOLD. Okay –

JERRY. And she had trouble talking about this stuff, she didn't even like talking to Stacey all that much, she was convinced that Stacey had it in for her –

ARNOLD. Jerry –

JERRY. And she – you know, she had real regrets. The last few years, I think she's been taking stock of everything, what she let my dad get away with, what she let *your* dad get away with –

ARNOLD. STOP.

(*Silence.* **ARNOLD** *breathes in and out.*)

JERRY. Buddy, I know there's a lot of shit here between us, I know you don't like me very much, but I don't know why we can't just *talk* –

ARNOLD. It's not that I don't like you! I mean I *don't* like you but that's not the issue, plenty of people don't like their siblings, they –

(*Just then, there is the sound of a door opening and some inaudible speaking in Arnold's flat.* **ARNOLD** *looks up.*)

Het gaat goed met me. Ech, het gaat goed met me. Laat me gewoon uitpraten.

(*Pause, listening.*)

Ik weet. Ik beloof.

(*Short pause.*)

Bedankt. Ik houd van je.

(*The sound of a door closing. Pause.*)

JERRY. Was that Bram?

(*Pause.*)

Tell him hi for me?

*(Silence. **ARNOLD** takes a breath.)*

ARNOLD. Jerry – I'm sorry, I thought I could do this, but – I can't. I'll look into this bill, I'll get in touch with the hospital, but I can't do – this. You and me.

(Pause.)

Okay?

(Pause.)

JERRY. Yeah, I –. I get it.

ARNOLD. Okay. Bye.

JERRY. But actually –! Sorry, I know you don't want to do this, but this is a little more – complicated than this one bill?

(Short pause.)

ARNOLD. Okay?

JERRY. In a way that it might be kinda hard to do this all over email. I think. Maybe.

ARNOLD. Jerry, just say it.

JERRY. She has a will.

(Short pause.)

ARNOLD. Really?

JERRY. Yeah I'll be goddamned, right?! Shocked me too. She can barely remember to pay the phone bill and the woman has a *will*. And anyway, she named me her health proxy which is why I've been dealing with the hospital and hospice, you know, but she also named an executor who has, like, power of attorney and access to bank accounts –

ARNOLD. Who is it?

(Pause. **JERRY** *hesitates, looking down.* **ARNOLD** *realizes.)*

ARNOLD. Wait –

JERRY. Yeah...

ARNOLD. You're saying *I'm* the –...?

(Short pause.)

That doesn't make any sense!

JERRY. Sure...

ARNOLD. I live in the *Netherlands*, we haven't spoken in years! Why would she do this?!

JERRY. Yeah I mean when she had this drawn up she knew I was going through some – shit, so maybe she just figured you'd be better at this. I mean you're the smarter one! Maybe it's a compliment!

ARNOLD. You emailed me saying you needed help with a *bill*, you didn't think this was the more important piece of business to address with me?!

JERRY. Yeah...

ARNOLD. I'm thousands of miles away, how can I –?!

JERRY. I talked to an estate lawyer guy, he said that this can all be done from afar.

(Pause.)

I mean, it's – what she wants? I guess?

(Silence. **ARNOLD** *lets out a sigh.)*

ARNOLD. God, one last middle finger before she dies, huh?

(Silence.)

JERRY. I'll make this as easy as possible, I promise!

(Pause.)

Okay?

Transition.

*(A few days later. **JERRY** and **ARNOLD** are now talking over video.)*

ARNOLD. Hi.

JERRY. *(Smiling.)* Hey there.

(Short pause.)

Look at you!

ARNOLD. What?

JERRY. No, just –. It's been a while since I've seen your face. You got old.

ARNOLD. Well you got *really* old.

JERRY. Sure did!

*(Awkward pause. **ARNOLD** looks at something on his computer.)*

ARNOLD. Anyway I don't know if you got my email yesterday but I talked with what's-her-name at the hospital –

JERRY. Candice! You remember Candy Apple!

ARNOLD. Uh-huh, I talked with her and there are *way* more unpaid bills than that one you got a couple weeks ago.

JERRY. Oh shit, really? More than the bill for thirty-five hundred?

ARNOLD. *Way* more. I'm looking at them right now. Do you want me to share my screen?

JERRY. I don't know what that means.

ARNOLD. Never mind. Anyway, something is obviously up with her Medicaid, I need to deal with that, but there are also just some really weird bills here, like – I'm trying to figure out what the deal is with this helicopter charge.

JERRY. Yeah, you know, the little rural-access hospital here didn't have the right, you know, the right facilities –

ARNOLD. I understand that, but why is there a charge for over eighteen grand for the helicopter? You told me she had helicopter insurance.

JERRY. Yeah, uh, turns out she stopped payin' for that a few years back. I guess she felt like she was wasting her money.

ARNOLD. Yeah, well, that sounds like her.

JERRY. And she didn't think she needed to worry about money because she had the, you know –

ARNOLD. The Giacometti.

JERRY. Uh-huh.

(**ARNOLD** *takes a long breath. He closes the document on his computer, rubbing his eyes.*)

I know it's late in Amsterdam, so if you'd rather do this tomorrow morning my time, I –

ARNOLD. We don't live in Amsterdam anymore.

(*Short pause.*)

JERRY. Oh.

ARNOLD. Bram got a new job at a museum in Rotterdam a couple years back.

(Pause.)

JERRY. That's, uh – that's still in Holland, though?

ARNOLD. Yeah. It's not that far. I mean, compared to Idaho nothing is far here.

JERRY. How is it?

*(Pause. **ARNOLD** takes a breath, deciding to engage.)*

ARNOLD. It's – fine. I miss Amsterdam, but it's only an hour or so by train.

JERRY. That's so cool. I'd still love to visit Europe sometime. Finally see another country.

ARNOLD. Uh-huh. I mean, you've been to Canada.

JERRY. What? I've never been to Canada.

ARNOLD. Yes you have. We took that boat thingy from Seattle to Victoria.

JERRY. What?

ARNOLD. We were in Seattle visiting Mom's cousin or something, and Mom wanted to see Victoria so we took the boat thing to Victoria for the day.

*(**JERRY** searches his memory.)*

JERRY. Are you *sure* that happened?

ARNOLD. Yeah, I'm sure. I was like eleven or twelve. It was a year or so after my dad left.

JERRY. Fuckin' hated that guy.

ARNOLD. Yeah, well. Me too.

JERRY. You know where he is now?

ARNOLD. I don't know, I think he's in Montana or something. He still leaves me a voicemail on my birthday, I don't call him back. What about Alan? Do you hear from him?

JERRY. Oh he died a couple years back.

ARNOLD. Oh. Shit, I –. Sorry, I didn't know.

JERRY. Oh it's fine, it's a miracle he lived as long as he did. He was pretty strung out at the end there.

ARNOLD. Did you at least get some money?

JERRY. Nah, he was still with Anita when he died. And she hates my guts, I'm never gonna see a penny. Think she already spent it anyway, the other day I saw that gold digger driving a brand-new F-150.

(Pause.)

I think I remember that trip to Seattle, but taking a boat to *Canada*?

ARNOLD. Yeah, we definitely did. I remember because you –...

*(Pause. **ARNOLD** stops himself.)*

JERRY. What?

ARNOLD. No, it's just... This is why I don't like talking about this stuff.

JERRY. What do you mean?

ARNOLD. It's like no matter what memory it is, no matter how seemingly innocuous it is, it always leads straight to shit. It's like being stuck in a maze and no matter what path you choose there's just black holes everywhere that you keep falling into.

(Pause.)

I remember because I went out on the deck and you came up behind me and picked me up and threatened to throw me overboard. And then I started crying, and you called me a little faggot. Then I peed myself, and Mom slapped me for that, and made me wear the pants for the rest of the day.

(Pause.)

JERRY. Oh.

(Pause.)

Guess I've – blocked some of that stuff out.

(Short pause.)

Sometimes I wonder, I just…

(**JERRY** *trails off.*)

ARNOLD. What?

JERRY. You're smarter than me, you remember things. Stuff sticks to you. But I've just never been like that. Maybe it's because I'm dumb, I don't know, I –…

(Pause.)

Mom came to me a few years back. She said she'd been thinking about – us, when we were kids. Turning a blind eye when my dad hit me, leaving you alone in the trailer for days at a time when she went on a bender, all that shit. And she – wanted me to forgive her. Maybe she knew that first stroke was coming.

(Short pause.)

And I had this weird reaction, I was so – caught off guard, I didn't know what to say. So I said, "Sure, Mom. I forgive you." But it was like, automatic, felt like a robot. I didn't feel like I forgave her, but I didn't feel angry either. And I thought about it later, and I thought – shouldn't I have felt *something*? And even now, I see her hooked up to all those machines, and I don't feel anything. And Stacey? When she told me she wanted to separate, I should of done something, I should have fought harder. I should be fighting harder right *now*, but –…

(Pause. **JERRY** *starts to become upset; he looks away.)*

*(***ARNOLD*** *looks at him. Pause.)*

ARNOLD. Jerry, I wanted to / ask –

JERRY. So how late is it?

(Short pause.)

ARNOLD. What?

JERRY. Over there in Amsterdam. Rotterdam.

ARNOLD. Oh, it's… I guess it's past midnight.

JERRY. Late.

ARNOLD. Yeah.

(Pause.)

Maybe you're right, maybe tomorrow is better.

JERRY. Sure. I can take care of this other stuff, you don't have to –. Sorry.

(Short pause.)

ARNOLD. I'll –.

(Pause.)

I'll be in touch.

(Pause.)

JERRY. Okay.

Transition.

*(Back on the video call. **JERRY** is carefully examining something. **ARNOLD** is a little uncomfortable.)*

JERRY. Wow.

(Pause.)

Wow, it's just –. Wow.

(Pause.)

It's really good!

ARNOLD. Thanks.

JERRY. Yeah the screen on my phone is kinda fucked up so it's hard to see, but it's really –. Wow.

ARNOLD. It's okay, you don't have / to –

JERRY. No, sorry, I sound like an idiot, I just don't have the –, you know. The *vocabulary* to talk about this stuff, you know –

ARNOLD. Well, you asked to see something.

JERRY. I used to be able to find your stuff on that website –

ARNOLD. Smit Gallery?

JERRY. Yeah, that one!

ARNOLD. I don't –... How did you find that?

JERRY. Oh I try to follow you however I can, you know. I hope that's not weird of me to do that.

ARNOLD. No, it's fine, I just – didn't know.

(Short pause.)

My stuff isn't there anymore.

JERRY. Oh yeah? How come?

ARNOLD. It doesn't matter, I just had a – falling out with –. It doesn't matter.

JERRY. I loved those little models you made, the ones of places from around here –

ARNOLD. Oh yeah, the Grangeville dioramas, they –. That was from a while ago. But yeah, people loved those. I mostly do paintings now –

JERRY. The tattoo parlor! You made a diorama of the tattoo parlor downtown!

ARNOLD. Yep.

JERRY. Those were so great. But I like this painting too, it's –! How come it says "roof"?

ARNOLD. Oh I –... I'm just interested in the ways that text can be incorporated into visual representation, the way it can both inform but also disrupt the work, it –... Never mind, what the fuck / am I doing?

JERRY. Oh no, sure I get it! Disrupting, I get that! Disrupting.

(Short pause.)

But so why does it say "roof"? And why is there a question mark after the word?

(Pause.)

ARNOLD. Um – I guess, it's about the idea of shelter? But in a – broader sense? The – tenuous things that are protecting us, giving us a sense of home.

JERRY. Oh! So like a house? Like a roof of a house.

(Pause.)

ARNOLD. Okay, it's nice that you wanted to see one of my paintings, but you don't have / to –

JERRY. It's really unsettled.

(Pause.)

ARNOLD. "Unsettled"?

JERRY. No, it's just – I don't know if that's the right word, but the whole painting, it just feels – unsettled, you know? That thing right here, it could almost be a body. Twisted, you know. But all these warm colors over here, it's like the guy is – out of reach of something, and –.

    (Pause.)

Fuck it, sorry. I don't know anything about art. I just like the painting.

    (Pause.)

ARNOLD. Have you –? Did you get the code yet?

JERRY. Oh, uh, lemme check...

    (He looks at something.)

Nope. The thing said it could take up to five minutes.

ARNOLD. Maybe you should try clicking the link again, get a new / code –

JERRY. It's only been a couple minutes, I'm sure it's coming.

    (Pause.)

Do you, uh – so do you like, have a new gallery where your stuff is at, or –?

ARNOLD. Uh – I have something coming up in a few months, in Utrecht.

JERRY. Oh, great!

ARNOLD. I mean it's not a solo exhibition, but / it –

JERRY. It's just amazing to me, the fact that you can make a living off this stuff.

(Catching himself.) Shit, I didn't mean / it like –

ARNOLD. Uh-huh.

JERRY. I just meant like, there's gotta be so many people out there, so many other artists – it's just so cool that you made it.

ARNOLD. Yep.

JERRY. And your painting, it's just so – you know, it's...

ARNOLD. Thanks.

JERRY. Shit, I don't –. I don't have the words, I'm sorry. I just – I know I wasn't exactly, like, *encouraging* all those years ago when you first talked about wanting to be an artist, and / I –

ARNOLD. Did you get it yet?

JERRY. Hm?

ARNOLD. The code. On Mom's phone. For / the –

JERRY. Oh right! Lemme... Yep, here it is.

*(Pause. **JERRY** reads something.)*

Okay, it's – five six eight three three four.

ARNOLD. *(Typing.)* Five six eight three three...

(Short pause.)

Okay, I'm in.

(Looking at the screen.) Wait, this is...? Are there any other accounts?

JERRY. No. Why?

*(**ARNOLD** continues to look at the numbers.)*

ARNOLD. This... This is bleak.

JERRY. How bleak?

ARNOLD. Like there's less than five grand in here. And the hospital bills alone are north of thirty.

JERRY. Oh shit.

ARNOLD. Yeah.

JERRY. Wait, are we gonna be, like, responsible for this?

ARNOLD. I don't –. I guess I don't know, I'm gonna have to talk to someone. Fuck.

JERRY. She would say stuff about living hand to mouth with her social security, but I thought she at least had savings.

ARNOLD. I mean I need to talk with Medicaid, but even if they cover the majority of it, there's –… Wait, what is –? What's this charge here for forty-five hundred dollars from last week?

JERRY. Oh, that's – down payment. For the funeral. I used her debit card. Woulda held off if I knew the account was that low.

    (Pause.)

Shit, should I have asked you first? I just figured –

ARNOLD. No, it's fine, I just… I didn't know you were / already –

JERRY. Well you said, last time we talked you were asking about this kinda stuff, I thought maybe it would be better to get on top of everything –

ARNOLD. No, it's –. This is good, I just didn't realize you were already organizing the funeral.

JERRY. I should have asked you about it first, I'm sorry –

ARNOLD. It's fine –

JERRY. Chaz over at the funeral home, he's a good guy. I talked to him about everything, I got the cheapest urn they had –

ARNOLD. You got the *cheapest* urn?

(Pause.)

JERRY. I just thought –. I thought that's what you wanted. You've been talking about saving money wherever we can –

ARNOLD. No, you're –. It's good, thank you.

(Pause.)

JERRY. You know Mom. This is what she would want. She hates people making a fuss.

ARNOLD. Uh-huh.

> (**ARNOLD** *goes back to the accounts on his screen.)*

JERRY. You remember that time Stacey tried throwin' her a surprise birthday party? I swear, I thought Mom was gonna punch her in the face –

ARNOLD. Did she own the lot or no?

JERRY. Whaddayoumean?

ARNOLD. The lot, in the trailer park, did she own it? Or was she leasing?

JERRY. Uh – she was leasing. *Is* leasing. She's still leasing.

ARNOLD. Why don't I see any payments over the last few months?

JERRY. I think Monty's been giving her a deal.

ARNOLD. A "deal"?

JERRY. I think he knew Mom didn't have much at all, I get the impression he hadn't been charging her for the last few years.

ARNOLD. Wait, he –? Jerry, you realize – if she was leasing then she had a contract, he could go after us for back payments if he wanted to –

JERRY. Oh Monty wouldn't do that.

ARNOLD. How do you know that?!

JERRY. They've known each other forever! I think they even went to high school together!

ARNOLD. That doesn't mean anything! There's a / contract –

JERRY. Oh c'mon, you know Monty, he would never go after us! Hell, I don't know if you remember this, but when you were like four or five, Mom and your dad disappeared to god knows where and he let us stay at his place for a few / nights –

ARNOLD. *Jerry please just –...*

(*Pause.*)

My point is, we need to sell the trailer as soon as we can. Even if we're not paying for the lot, there's still utilities, taxes... I'm sure we won't get much for it, but we need whatever we can get now –

JERRY. Yeah, well – I mean I can start looking into that, but it's –...

(*Short pause.*)

ARNOLD. What?

JERRY. It's not a big deal, I can figure it out, it's just that – I'm sorta staying there. In the trailer.

(*Pause.*)

ARNOLD. Since when?

JERRY. Moved in a few months ago to help Mom out. It's not permanent or anything, just for a while so Stacey and I can figure things out.

(*Pause.* **ARNOLD** *shifts uncomfortably.*)

ARNOLD. Wait, are you – there right now?

JERRY. Yeah. In our old bedroom. You couldn't tell? Hank next door, he doesn't have a password on his wifi.

(Short pause.)

Here, I can show you the place on the / wall where –

ARNOLD. *No, I –.* No thank you.

(ARNOLD pauses, taking a few deep breaths.)

JERRY. I know it may sound weird, but it's been sorta helpful? I think I said this the other day but I don't remember stuff all that well, and staying here has, like, reminded me of a lot of stuff, some of it good but a lot of it not so great, and / it –

ARNOLD. Okay I'm glad that it's been, you know, *helpful* for you and I'm glad that you're unpacking some of this stuff, but if you need someone to talk to, it shouldn't be me.

JERRY. Okay, / sorry –

ARNOLD. I'm just saying, it's great that you're working out some stuff, it really is. But if you need someone to talk to, you should talk to a professional, like a therapist –

JERRY. I have a therapist.

(Pause.)

ARNOLD. You do?

JERRY. Few months now. You know, it's been – helpful.

(Pause. ARNOLD doesn't know how to respond.)

I'm not saying I'm a different person, but maybe I'm – not the *same* person?

(Pause.)

ARNOLD. Did something – happen?

(Pause.)

JERRY. Eh – nothing, really.

(Pause.)

ARNOLD. Really?

JERRY. Just started to become pretty damn clear that I needed to do something. Dr. Gatterbein, she – that's her name – she says that I shouldn't expect anything from you. So you know, I don't expect anything from you.

ARNOLD. You – talk to her about me?

JERRY. A little. It's been – good for me, I think? Just to talk things through. Dr. Gatterbein says it's good to put everything in context. To better understand – everything. Why I did the stuff I did.

*(Pause. **ARNOLD** stares at him.)*

ARNOLD. What "context" is that, exactly?

JERRY. Oh, just – you know, my dad, the –. You know, all the stuff that went on with him and me. Before you were around, she talks about how I didn't have any positive male role models, and that –. So you know, that's one of the reasons why I thought it was okay to pick on you like that. I know it's fucked up, but it was my way of – trying.

*(Short pause. **ARNOLD** seethes.)*

ARNOLD. "Trying"?

JERRY. I mean when you were like eleven, twelve, I started to realize that you were probably gay, or at least just sensitive, and Grangeville High could be pretty rough-and-tumble back then and I wanted to make sure you could, you know. Hold your own if someone –

ARNOLD. You know what? I think I'm done.

(*Pause.*)

JERRY. I'm sorry.

ARNOLD. No, I'm serious, I think I'm done here.

JERRY. I'm *sorry*, okay? But if you wanna go, we can talk tomorrow –

ARNOLD. No, you're not hearing me, I said I'm *done*. I don't care that she named me executor, I'm not doing this anymore. So you can just figure this out by yourself and leave me the fuck alone.

(*Pause.*)

JERRY. You can't –, you can't do that –

ARNOLD. No, actually, I *can* do that. I looked it up and the court can just appoint someone else.

JERRY. You mean me?

ARNOLD. I don't care.

(*Pause.* **JERRY** *scoffs.*)

JERRY. Yeah, well that fuckin' [makes sense]...

(*Pause.*)

ARNOLD. 'Scuse me?

JERRY. I guess it makes sense, since you left me back here to take care of her all these years.

ARNOLD. Oh fuck you, you could have left whenever you wanted –

JERRY. Oh yeah?! And then who was gonna take care of Mom? She stopped driving over ten years ago, who do you think was taking her to the doctor and buying her groceries?

ARNOLD. You could have put her in a retirement home, or –

JERRY. With what money?! Only option would be to put her in the county care place, she would have been *miserable* there –

ARNOLD. Okay, you know what? I'm not responsible for your shitty life decisions! You made the choice to stay in Grangeville, get married, have kids, take care of Mom –

JERRY. Well we can't all be like you, Arnie! Not all of us can just blow outta town and move to fuckin' Europe –!

ARNOLD. I got out of there *despite* you. Have you fucking forgotten that?!

(*Silence.*)

JERRY. Okay, just –. I'm sorry, I –

(**ARNOLD** *ends the video call and, for the first time, exits the stage.* **JERRY** *is left alone.*)

(*Silence.*)

(*Finally:*) Are you –? You still there?

(*Pause.*)

I don't –. I don't really use these video call thingies ever so I don't know if you're still there.

(*Silence.*)

Arnie? *Please.*

(*No response.*)

Transition.

(**ARNOLD** *reenters.* **JERRY** *and* **ARNOLD** *both pull out their phones, looking at them. We hear the sound of nearby highway traffic throughout the scene. For the first time, they share the same physical space.)*

JERRY. The weekend of the fifth is fine? I'd just have to hand him off to you before like five or so –

ARNOLD. We're out of town that weekend.

JERRY. You are? Where?

ARNOLD. Spokane, I told you. Tom has a swim meet. Lauren's gonna meet us there, I've already got the motel booked.

JERRY. Why isn't it on the calendar?

ARNOLD. I told you about it when we talked last week, I / said –

JERRY. Sorry, I don't –. You're the one that says we should be putting everything on the calendar –

ARNOLD. Okay, sorry. I messed up. What about the weekend of the twelfth?

JERRY. I work that weekend.

ARNOLD. Well you can still see him at night?

JERRY. The whole point of this is that I get to spend time with him, Stacey, I don't –

(*A loud horn in the background startles* **JERRY**, *cutting him off.)*

ARNOLD. Well why are you booking weekend shifts?

JERRY. I told you, I have to do at least *some* weekends, those are the big sale days. Not too many people buyin' RVs on a Tuesday morning. Look, can't I just take him next week?

ARNOLD. The whole week?

JERRY. Why not?

(**ARNOLD** *looks away.*)

ARNOLD. I mean, maybe. You should ask him.

(*Short pause.*)

JERRY. What?

(*Pause.*)

ARNOLD. Tom told me he doesn't want to spend more than a couple days with you at a time.

JERRY. He –? What, is he mad at me, or –?

ARNOLD. It's not you, Jerry. It's that trailer. He hates staying in that thing.

JERRY. He told you that?

ARNOLD. Every Monday when he comes home.

JERRY. Well what's wrong with it?

ARNOLD. C'mon. Sleeping on a cot in his grandma's old trailer?

JERRY. Well I can get him a bed if he –

ARNOLD. It's more than just the bed, Jerry. It's – depressing as hell.

JERRY. Well I could – paint the bedroom or something, or –?

(*Another horn startles* **JERRY.***)

Goddammit! Why are we doin' this here?!

ARNOLD. You were the one who wanted to do this in person, I said we coulda done this over the phone.

JERRY. It's just better to do this in person, I think, the phone is so – I don't know. I don't like it.

ARNOLD. Well, you wanted to meet in person.

JERRY. Yeah, but outside of a damn *gas station*? We could've gotten a meal or something, why couldn't we just meet at Seasons?

ARNOLD. Because we'd know everybody there. And knowing us, we'd get to shouting sooner or later. And I don't need half the town knowin' our business.

JERRY. I'm not ashamed of anything.

ARNOLD. I'm not sayin' I'm *ashamed*, I just don't need people knowin' our business.

(Pause. They look at each other.)

JERRY. Well, anyway. It's good to see you. You look good.

(Pause.)

Are you good?

(Pause.)

ARNOLD. Yeah, uh –. Pretty good, actually.

(Pause.)

How 'bout you?

JERRY. Uh – you know.

ARNOLD. How's your mom doin'?

JERRY. Pretty much the same. Still not waking up.

ARNOLD. Do her doctors think she will, or –?

JERRY. I don't think they know.

(Pause.)

ARNOLD. You've been talking with Arnie, then?

(Short pause.)

JERRY. Little bit.

ARNOLD. Huh. And how's that been?

JERRY. Not – great. I actually haven't heard from him in a few weeks. He hasn't responded to my texts.

(Pause.)

C'mon, Stace. Let me buy you lunch. We don't have to get into the shit, we can just catch up.

ARNOLD. I would, but I got something later. Book club.

JERRY. *Book club?* Seriously?

ARNOLD. Yeah. Dana pulled me into it. It's alright.

JERRY. Book club, geez. What are you reading?

ARNOLD. It's like a – history book. It's about the Middle Ages.

JERRY. You're readin' a textbook?

ARNOLD. No, it's – whatdotheycallit. Popular History.

JERRY. Why the hell would you wanna read a book about the Middle Ages?

ARNOLD. It's interesting! For real! I know it sounds boring but it's really fascinating, readin' about how people lived back then.

JERRY. You read the whole thing?

ARNOLD. *(Defensive.) Yes.*

(Short pause.)

Most of it. I mean I skimmed some of the boring parts but I got the gist of the whole thing.

JERRY. That's – cool. Didn't know you were into that kinda thing.

ARNOLD. Yeah, me either. But it's been – good. Met a lot of new people, too. Some people make the drive in from Lewiston.

JERRY. Oh yeah?

ARNOLD. One of them is even a professor. Adjunct professor, whatever.

JERRY. Of Literature?

ARNOLD. Sports Communication. But still, he's a professor.

JERRY. Huh. Neat.

ARNOLD. Yeah. I guess, I'm just startin' to get pretty aware that Tom is gonna be outta the house in two years. Wondering what's after that.

(Short pause.)

JERRY. Oh yeah?

ARNOLD. Yeah, I don't know. I mean I've never loved working for Duane, he's nice and everything but – how interesting can working for a CPA actually be?

JERRY. Yeah, well. I'm sure there's other jobs to be had around here.

ARNOLD. Yeah, or... I don't know.

*(Pause. **JERRY** looks at him.)*

JERRY. What?

ARNOLD. Oh, just – you know. I don't *need* to stay in Grangeville.

(Pause.)

JERRY. Wait – what?

ARNOLD. I don't know? I've been here all my life, once Tom is gone there's nothing really keeping me here.

JERRY. Wait, you're gonna *leave*?

ARNOLD. Well, I'd wanna make sure Tom is settled in school or whatever, but – maybe. Lauren's just fine on her own. Hell, she's practically encouraging me to get outta here.

JERRY. Well where the hell would you go?

ARNOLD. Oh, I don't know. It's just a thought.

JERRY. Seriously, where?!

ARNOLD. I don't know! Oregon? California? New Zealand, Denmark, fucking Antarctica! I don't know!

(**JERRY** *scoffs, looking away.*)

JERRY. Fuckin' just *running away*.

ARNOLD. 'Scuse me?

JERRY. I mean my god, you act as if running off, leaving everything behind is some kind of *solution*, like you can just turn your back on everything / and –

ARNOLD. The hell are you talking about? What "solution"? You saying I got a problem?

JERRY. What about your dad?

ARNOLD. Sherry's here! He's not alone!

JERRY. So you'll just pawn him off onto your sister, just like –...

(*Pause.*)

ARNOLD. Okay. So this is about Arnold.

JERRY. No –

ARNOLD. Yes, this is very *clearly* about your brother.

JERRY. Half brother.

ARNOLD. You know, no one forced you to stay here. No one forced you to move into your mom's trailer.

JERRY. Well what the hell else was I supposed to do?!

ARNOLD. You could've hired someone! Home health aide, something –

JERRY. So invite some stranger into her home, someone who'd probably skim outta her jewelry box when she's sleeping, that's what I should've done?

ARNOLD. What jewelry?! Did your mom have some diamond brooches squirreled away that I don't know about?!

JERRY. You know what I / mean –

ARNOLD. And why are you still staying in that trailer?! God, your mom has been in the hospital for months now, you're just staying in there keeping things exactly the same, as if she's gonna come back home someday –

JERRY. You're right, Stacey. Better to just burn the thing down now. And maybe you could help me pull the plug on my mom, maybe that would make things easier.

ARNOLD. Oh for Christ's sake, I can't do this again –!

JERRY. She's my mom, dammit. And he's your dad. That *means something*.

(*Pause.*)

Sorry, it's just –. This is lot to take in, Stace.

(*Short pause.*)

ARNOLD. Listen, Jer. You don't have to stay here either, you know. Not to be a downer, but I doubt your mom's gonna be around much longer. You really wanna just hang out in that trailer for the rest of your life?

JERRY. No. I wanna move back home.

(**ARNOLD**'s *head falls into his chest.*)

ARNOLD. Oh my god, please don't do this / again –

JERRY. I just don't see the point in calling it quits like this, we can work this out!

ARNOLD. There's nothing to work out. That's the thing.

(*Pause.*)

I don't hate you, Jer. I just don't want to be married to you anymore.

JERRY. But what if that changes?

ARNOLD. It's *not*. I'm not trying to hurt you, but that's not gonna change.

JERRY. But what about –?

(*Short pause.*)

What if I still wanna be married to you? Isn't that something?

(*Pause.*)

ARNOLD. Sure, it's something. But it's a you thing. Not a me thing.

(**JERRY** *takes a long breath. Silence.*)

JERRY. Gimme a cigarette.

ARNOLD. No.

JERRY. Stacey, c'mon, it's *one cigarette* –

ARNOLD. I don't have one! I'm on the patch.

(*Pause.* **JERRY** *deflates.*)

JERRY. Oh god...

ARNOLD. Six weeks now. Two slipups. But I only had one each time and I threw away the rest of the pack.

(Short pause.)

JERRY. I'm sorry. I –. Lately it just feels like the ground below me is turning into water. And I'm about to sink.

(Short pause.)

ARNOLD. Look, we have two kids together. We're never gonna be strangers. And I know it's hard with your mom, but we all go through that sooner or later. Nothin's turning to water. And your mom's trailer isn't a lifeboat.

*(**JERRY** smirks at him.)*

JERRY. You come up with that metaphor all on your own?

ARNOLD. Yep. On the spot. It's that book club, it's making me all literary.

(Pause.)

But you're, not –... I mean you're not thinking again / about –

JERRY. *No*, Stace.

ARNOLD. I'm just making sure! 'Cause you were talkin' this way when you tried / to –

JERRY. I didn't *try*, I –. Dr. Gatterbein says it was a, whattayoucallit. Passive attempt.

ARNOLD. Well you left a damn note, that doesn't feel all / that –

JERRY. Stace, please don't –. I have my therapist. I'm on solid ground. I'm just – unhappy. That's different. And I don't know, I just wish Arnie would – let me in.

(Pause.)

ARNOLD. Look, Jer, I don't know what to tell you here. The way you treated him when he was still living here –

JERRY. I was just –! I was just trying to toughen him up, I wasn't –! Dr. Gatterbein / says –

ARNOLD. By "toughen him up" do you mean beat the *shit* out of him?

(**JERRY** *looks away, ashamed. Silence.*)

JERRY. Yeah. That's probably a more accurate way to put it.

(*Pause.*)

I'm not saying I didn't mess up a *ton*, believe me, but – it wasn't all like that. There were plenty of times I would let him stay at my apartment when his dad was drunk or when Mom blew outta town for days at a time. And when he was little he didn't have a ton of friends, so there were plenty of nights my buddies would be out drinking but I'd be in the trailer with Arnie playing cards. Letting him win.

(*Short pause.*)

I just wish he could remember that stuff, too. It's like he's taken the worst parts of me, and he's just decided that it's all that I am.

(*Pause.*)

ARNOLD. Yeah, well. If I were him, I think I'd be more hung up on you beating him up than those card games you let him win.

(*Pause.* **JERRY** *thinks.*)

JERRY. Yeah...

(*Pause.*)

ARNOLD. What do you *actually* wanna say to him?

JERRY. I don't know –

ARNOLD. Seriously!

(Pause. **JERRY** *relents, thinking for a moment, then looks at* **ARNOLD**.*)*

JERRY. I guess, I'd wanna say... I was jealous of you. I know that wasn't an excuse. But I was a shit brother.

ARNOLD. Half brother.

JERRY. I was a shit half brother.

ARNOLD. Yes, you were.

JERRY. And it's not up to me, of course, it's up to you, but I'd like – to try again? Just to, you know. Make sense of everything. It just feels like, with Mom on her way out, I wanna – figure this stuff out.

(Pause.)

ARNOLD. *(Thinking.)* Hm.

(Pause. **ARNOLD** *thinks.)*

You know, this book I'm reading? About the Middle Ages? There's something about it, reading about all these people who lived eight hundred or so years ago, which is – if you think about it – not that long? That's like, what, ten or twelve human lifetimes stacked on top of each other?

JERRY. Yeah?

ARNOLD. And you read about how people lived back then, sleeping on piles of hay, drinking dirty water, disease, war, torture, all of it. I think nowadays we wanna believe that suffering leads us somewhere, like we have to go through the shit in order to get to the good stuff. Like there's some reward at the end. But most of the time? Suffering is just like – pfffft. Just happens. And all these people? No one apologized to them for all the shit they went through. They just had to go through it, and then die.

(Pause.)

JERRY. Jesus, Stacey, that's like the most depressing thing I've ever heard. Should you be reading this book?

ARNOLD. No no no, the point is – there's freedom in that! It means that we can't be sitting around waiting for the world to reward us or forgive us or even give us a *reason* for all of it. So all the shit we've been through, all the shit that we've done, or that other people have done to us, it doesn't *have* to mean anything. Sometimes there's no reason. Sometimes it's all just – shit that's hanging around in our toilet, and we can either sit there and stare at it or just – flush it.

(Pause.)

JERRY. That metaphor is fuckin' gross, Stace.

ARNOLD. They can't all be winners.

*(Pause. **JERRY** takes a long breath.)*

I should think about taking off. I told 'em I'd pick up plates and cups from the Family Dollar.

JERRY. Where's your book club?

ARNOLD. Sherry's place.

JERRY. *Sherry* is in a book club?

ARNOLD. She's trying to screw the Sports Communication professor.

JERRY. Got it.

ARNOLD. I'll talk to Tom, we'll figure out a weekend. Okay?

*(**JERRY** nods, looking away. Pause.)*

I know you wanna talk with your brother, Jer. I know it's eating at you. But also, you might have to get used to the idea that – he just might not want to? Ever? I mean if had a brother who treated me like that as a kid, I'm not sure I'd want a relationship with him either.

(Pause.)

ARNOLD. And listen, you need to get the *fuck* outta that trailer. I'm sure it's just making things worse.

JERRY. Where am I supposed to go?

(They look at each other.)

Transition.

(The sunlight begins to fade into night as **ARNOLD** *and* **JERRY** *continue to look at each other.* **JERRY** *speaks in a slight Dutch accent.)*

ARNOLD. This is – nice.

(Short pause.)

This is nice, right?

JERRY. Yes, it's –. It's nice.

ARNOLD. It's been a while since I made us a proper dinner.

JERRY. Just a few weeks.

ARNOLD. That's a long time for us. Ten years ago I was cooking you two meals a day every day.

JERRY. Well, that was ten years ago.

(Pause.)

ARNOLD. Maybe you could stay at home tonight? With me?

JERRY. Arnold –

ARNOLD. I'm not pressuring you.

JERRY. It's really not –. I have an early meeting tomorrow with the board, if I sleep at the studio I can spend more time in the morning preparing.

ARNOLD. Another one?

JERRY. There's just – a lot going on at the moment. It's good, the Education department is expanding, it's exciting, but it's just busy at the moment.

ARNOLD. I mean if you wanted to stay you could always just take a car in the morning, I could make you breakfast / while you –

JERRY. Let's just –. This is nice, right? Right now? Can't we – let this be nice?

> (**ARNOLD** *takes a breath, nodding his head.*)

Did you try the white?

ARNOLD. I'm okay.

JERRY. It's good, I got it for you, it's the one you like, the pinot gris / from –

ARNOLD. I'm okay, Bram.

JERRY. You're allowed to have a glass of wine.

ARNOLD. I know, I just don't want one.

> *(Pause.)*

JERRY. Have you been able to get work done here?

ARNOLD. Yeah, it's okay.

JERRY. You should use the studio if you like. When I'm at work it's just sitting there empty –

ARNOLD. It's fine, I'll – give you your space. That's what we said. And I'm fine here, I'm all set up at this point.

JERRY. Do you – have any new pieces, or –?

ARNOLD. Uh – they're sort of in progress, I guess? I don't know. I can't figure out if I'm doing the actual pieces or if I'm just making things in order to get to the actual pieces.

JERRY. What have you shown to Eline?

ARNOLD. I'm – close. To showing her something.

> (*Pause.*)

JERRY. Wait, you haven't –?

ARNOLD. I've talked her through the ideas, she's not gonna be surprised or / anything –

JERRY. How the hell did you get her to agree to include you in the show before she's even seen anything?

ARNOLD. She's known my stuff for fifteen years now, I think at this point she trusts me –

JERRY. That's just – *very* unlike her. Which is good! It's good, she has faith in you.

ARNOLD. Yeah, it's –. It's good.

> (*Pause.*)

JERRY. Can I see?

ARNOLD. You absolutely cannot.

JERRY. Oh, c'mon.

ARNOLD. No! You'll do that thing.

JERRY. What thing?

ARNOLD. You know, you'll look at it and you'll say something cryptic or you'll say half a sentence and then I'll spend the next week wondering what you were about / to say –

JERRY. Oh my god.

ARNOLD. Seriously! You'll look at it and you'll say something like, "It feels a little...?" And then you'll stop yourself and you won't say anything else and I'll quietly go insane wondering what the fuck you were going to say.

JERRY. You're too sensitive.

ARNOLD. And you're too glib.

JERRY. "Glib"? I don't know that word.

ARNOLD. Oh, like – I don't know. Like careless, or –

JERRY. You're saying I'm careless?!

ARNOLD. No it's not that bad, that's not the right equivalent, it's –. I don't know the Dutch word for it... "Vlug" maybe?

JERRY. That just means "rapid."

ARNOLD. I don't know! I don't –. Just forget it. It's not important. Just give me a few weeks, I'll show you something then. And you can rip my ego to shreds.

JERRY. I look forward to it.

 (Pause.)

I was cleaning out the studio the other day. I found some of your old pieces from that exhibition you did in The Hague? The Grangeville dioramas?

ARNOLD. Jesus, we still have those? That was, what, twelve years ago?

JERRY. Thirteen, I looked it up. There's only a couple, I'm surprised they didn't sell –

ARNOLD. Which ones are they?

JERRY. There was the, what's the word, the pawnshop?

ARNOLD. Uh-huh.

JERRY. And the, you know, the ice cream restaurant –

ARNOLD. Dairy Queen.

JERRY. Yeah, that's it. They're so good!

ARNOLD. Do me a favor and throw them out.

JERRY. Are you kidding? These are important, your early work! You can sell them in twenty years, there's your retirement.

ARNOLD. *(Chuckling.)* Right.

JERRY. You always spoke about making a diorama of your childhood home, that would have been fantastic. You should still do that!

ARNOLD. Yeah, Mom's trailer is a little – too close to home.

(Short pause.)

The sad thing is that diorama would probably bring in more money than anything I've made in the last ten years. Making fun of America, it's the one theme in modern European art that is consistently evergreen.

JERRY. You weren't making fun.

ARNOLD. I know. But you make little models of Dairy Queens and strip malls and rural highways, suddenly you're critiquing late-stage American imperialism. I thought I was just showing people things from where I grew up.

JERRY. Well, people liked them.

ARNOLD. Yeah, for a while. I was a fascination, this bumpkin from Idaho who didn't go to any of the right schools. I could only coast on that for so long.

JERRY. That's a bit of an oversimplification –

ARNOLD. Really? You think it's a coincidence that once I started doing more serious stuff everyone lost interest? As long as I'm making dioramas of gas stations I'm fine, the moment I try something else they all remembered I didn't go to the Sorbonne.

JERRY. Okay, / okay –

ARNOLD. They want this narrative of the scrappy damaged American crawling himself up the ladder from a Communications major at a state school, excavating the tacky landscapes of his childhood –

JERRY. Or maybe people just didn't like your newer work?

(**ARNOLD** *takes a deep breath, shifting uncomfortably.*)

(*Pause.*)

I'm not saying you're newer stuff isn't good, / I just –

ARNOLD. I get it.

JERRY. You know, your early work, it just felt very – big. Your newer work is just more personal, it's more – specific to you, your emotional life.

(*Short pause.*)

Speaking of which...

ARNOLD. (*Sighing.*) Bram –

JERRY. I'm allowed to ask.

(*Pause.*)

ARNOLD. I haven't talked to him in a few weeks, okay? I just don't need to be, like, fodder for his fuckin' therapy sessions or whatever.

JERRY. Is it so terrible he's in therapy?

ARNOLD. No, it's fine, it's – whatever, it's probably a good thing. For his kids, at least. But I don't need to like, be a part of it. He's taken enough from me over the years.

JERRY. He's trying.

(**ARNOLD** *looks at him.*)

ARNOLD. What are you doing?

JERRY. I'm not doing / anything –

ARNOLD. I'm not –. I don't know why we're even talking about him –

JERRY. I was mostly curious about your mother. Do you know how she's doing?

(*Pause.*)

ARNOLD. I told Jerry that if anything changes, he should get in touch with me.

JERRY. So you don't know.

ARNOLD. Okay, again, what are you / doing?

JERRY. I just –. Jesus, I really didn't want to / do this –

ARNOLD. You're the one who brought up my family –

JERRY. Don't you think you should *deal* with this? In real life? You at least used to deal with it in your art, but nowadays you don't even do that, you just paint these these these depressing meditations –

ARNOLD. Wow. Okay then.

(*Pause.* **JERRY** *takes a breath.*)

JERRY. I didn't mean it like that, I –

ARNOLD. That's how you think of my stuff now?

JERRY. No, I –! Dammit, Arnold, it's just English, you know it's hard for me to do this in English, everything comes out blunt –

ARNOLD. Well it doesn't sound like there was much lost in translation there.

JERRY. I don't know why I'm the one who has to do this. This shouldn't be my job!

(*Silence.* **ARNOLD** *takes a breath.*)

ARNOLD. Okay, Bram, I'm sorry. I'm being a dick. I'm sorry.

(*Pause.*)

I made dessert?

(*Pause.*)

JERRY. You *made* it?

ARNOLD. I bought it, whatever.

(*Pause.* **JERRY** *smiles a little despite himself.*)

JERRY. It just feels as if, sometimes, you make a choice to – torture yourself. And I think sometimes you think that's what an artist does? But it's – so unnecessary. This trope of the suffering artist, it's so silly and tired.

ARNOLD. This coming from the guy who's early work included droplets of his own blood.

JERRY. Yeah, exactly, I was twenty-two and I was an idiot. And what are you talking about, "early work"? It's my *only* work.

ARNOLD. I still think you should start working again.

JERRY. I *do* work.

ARNOLD. That's not what I –. You know what I mean.

JERRY. I think you're artistic enough for both of us. Anyway. I just liked the idea of being an artist, I didn't like actually making art. That's not very sustainable.

(*Silence.*)

ARNOLD. There's just something about talking with him. Jerry. Whenever I see his face, and he –... And it's not like, conjuring bad memories or anything, I feel like at this point in my life I've dealt with all that. It's more like – I don't want to be that person anymore, his brother. I just *don't want to be his brother.*

(*Pause.*)

JERRY. I'm not sure it works that way?

ARNOLD. Well why not? I mean, I *am* a completely different person. I live in a different country, I'm twenty years older, my fuckin' organs have grown entirely new cells –

JERRY. Okay, let's stay on earth, / Arnold –

ARNOLD. I'm serious! I'm not just pontificating, I'm saying I can choose who I am. And if I'm not his brother, then he's just some guy out in Idaho. And she's some dying old lady. Same as any dying old lady anywhere else on the planet, at any time in history or the future. Bodies in the ground.

JERRY. She's not in the ground yet.

(Pause.)

I should go soon. I want to go over my notes for tomorrow's meeting before bed. We're adding four new programs this year, did I tell you that?

ARNOLD. Four? Holy shit.

JERRY. Yeah. And this is my one chance to convince them that we need to make a new hire in the Education department.

ARNOLD. They ask too much of you. What if they don't approve another hire?

JERRY. I'll figure it out.

ARNOLD. Seriously, they can't keep doing this / to you –

JERRY. Well we have to get money somehow.

*(Pause. **ARNOLD** looks away.)*

I / didn't –

ARNOLD. No, I get it.

JERRY. Don't make this about you, I wasn't talking about / you –

ARNOLD. I said I get it.

(Pause.)

I'm still getting my teaching resume together –

JERRY. You said that three months ago.

> *(Pause.)*

Okay, I really need to go.

ARNOLD. You know, you don't have to keep working at the museum.

> *(Pause. **JERRY** looks at him, speechless.)*

You haven't been happy there for over a year now. You say it all the time.

JERRY. I do not –. I *complain* about the job, like a normal person who complains about work, but I don't want / to –

ARNOLD. I'm just saying, there's nothing keeping us from moving back to Amsterdam. We were happier there, all our friends are there! Ever since we moved, things have just gone / to shit –

JERRY. Okay, I do *not* have time for this discussion / at this moment.

ARNOLD. I could do private lessons, we could find a cheaper flat so you wouldn't have to find a new job immediately. Hell, I could work at a café if I really needed to.

JERRY. A *café*? Jesus, Arnold, we're in our *forties* –

ARNOLD. I don't care! I'm sick of it here, at least in Amsterdam there's a sense of history, it's not some town that got leveled in World War II and replaced with fuckin' shipping containers and brutalist McDonald's –

JERRY. Come back to earth, Arnold!

ARNOLD. And you've said yourself that the museum doesn't value you like they should, is that really reason enough for us / to –?

JERRY. They're talking about making me director.

(Pause.)

ARNOLD. Director?

JERRY. Caroline is retiring next year. And she wants me to take over as Education and Audience Director. And the board seems to agree.

(Pause.)

ARNOLD. How long have you known?

JERRY. A few months now.

ARNOLD. *Months?!* Why didn't you tell me?!

JERRY. Because I knew how you would react. For years now you've been acting as if my job at the museum is some day job, something I'm doing before I start painting again, but I've been telling you for years now, this *is* my job! This is what I want, I'm happy there! And if this works out I'll probably start making close to twice what I'm making now –

ARNOLD. Look, if this is about money, I can find work, I can start bringing in more / money –

JERRY. You're not hearing me, this isn't about money. I don't care about the money!

ARNOLD. Yeah, well. Of course you don't care about money.

(Short pause.)

JERRY. What is that supposed to mean?

ARNOLD. Both of your parents were doctors, Bram. Only kids who grew up with money get to say things like, "I don't care about money."

JERRY. That's not –! Oh my god, it's like shooting clay pigeons with you, I can't keep track of your grievances! Arnold, I could never understand what it is to have your childhood, an abusive brother and a mother who did everything for her shitty husbands and nothing for her kids. But I can't change that! And I am exactly where I want to be in my life. I like my job, it's secure, it has good pay, good holiday allowance, good pension. And you're talking about moving back to Amsterdam and working at a *café*? We are – *oceans* apart, Arnold, we...

(*Short pause.*)

You want to know why people liked your earlier work? Because it was vibrant and fun and audacious, because *you* were vibrant and fun and audacious. But over the years you and your work, you've both become so *hardened*...

You choose to forget this, but you were even more miserable in Amsterdam. Because these "friends" you're talking about were just other artists whose shows you would attend just so you could, I don't know, what's the word, *stew* on the fact that it's someone else's show and not yours, like you're the victim, like you're *seeking* this this this, I don't know the English, *kruisiging* –

ARNOLD. Crucifixion.

JERRY. Yes! You put yourself on this cross, for what reason?! I don't know why you do this, you put yourself at a distance from me, you blame Rotterdam, you blame your upbringing. You blame the art scene, but maybe?! Maybe the real problem is you! Maybe *you're* the problem, and I can't fix you, and maybe I need to stop fucking *trying*, and –...

(**JERRY** *stops himself, taking a few deep breaths. Silence.*)

(**ARNOLD** *stares at the ground.*)

(*Finally:*) This is –... We shouldn't do this tonight.

(*Pause.*)

JERRY. I do love you, Arnold. That hasn't changed. But you need to come back to me.

>   (*Pause.*)

I need to go.

>   (*Pause.* **ARNOLD** *continues to stare at the ground.*)

Arnold?

>   (*Pause.*)

ARNOLD. Okay.

>   (**JERRY** *leaves the stage.* **ARNOLD** *is left alone for the first time. He stares forward.*)

Transition.

>   (*Slowly, the light begins to shift as we hear Arnold's phone buzz.*)

>   (**JERRY** *reenters. It's late where* **ARNOLD** *is; it's clear he has been drinking.*)

>   (**ARNOLD** *answers.*)

ARNOLD. Hey.

JERRY. Oh, hey – Arnie?

ARNOLD. Yeah?

JERRY. I'm glad you –. Sorry I didn't think you were gonna answer –

ARNOLD. Why are you calling me?

>   (*Pause.*)

JERRY. I – haven't heard from you in a while, I sent you that text a few weeks back but you never wrote me / back –

ARNOLD. Yeah, I just –. I've been busy, you know.

JERRY. Oh, sure –

ARNOLD. I was trying to get some pieces together for a show, this –. But it's just not – you know. It's been rough, I can't seem to focus, or –.

(*Short pause.*)

Maybe I should go back to making dioramas again?

(*Pause.*)

Anyway, I told Bram I had this big show –

JERRY. Okay –

ARNOLD. I told him that Eline was including me in her next show.

JERRY. That's – good –

ARNOLD. Yeah, well, she –. She actually just said she would *look* at my stuff. But I – don't think I have anything to show her. I mean, I have – stuff? But it's – shitty. I'm pretty sure it's shitty.

(*Pause.*)

Maybe I should do dioramas. Maybe that's my problem.

(*Pause.*)

JERRY. You been drinking, Arnie?

ARNOLD. You taught me well.

(*This stings.* **JERRY** *looks down. Pause.*)

JERRY. Is Bram there, can he –?

ARNOLD. Bram's gone.

JERRY. Where is he?

ARNOLD. I don't know. He's been sleeping in my studio for
the last two months.

(*Pause.*)

JERRY. Oh –

ARNOLD. He says he's figuring some stuff out. Or I need
to figure some stuff out. Everyone needs to figure out
some stuff apparently!

JERRY. Have you –? Maybe you should give him a call –

ARNOLD. We haven't talked in weeks. Because by this
point I'm sure he's seen Eline's announcement, so by
this point he knows I am *not* in the show that I told
him I was going to be in. And I don't know how to talk
to him now.

(*Pause.*)

JERRY. Why are you tellin' me all this, Arnie?

ARNOLD. I don't know. I seriously don't know. Because it
doesn't matter anymore, I guess?

(*Pause.*)

Okay, I need –. I should go to bed. It's late here, I –

JERRY. Mom died, Arnie.

(*Silence.* **ARNOLD** *stares forward.*)

ARNOLD. Oh.

(*Pause.*)

When?

JERRY. Last night, sometime. They think she probably
had another stroke.

(Pause.)

Arnie?

(Pause.)

ARNOLD. Yeah, I –. I'm here.

(Pause.)

JERRY. Everything's – taken care of. Stace is on her way over right now, she's gonna help me with getting everything in here organized. And she helped me sort out the stuff with Medicaid, so we're all good there. So there's –, you know. You don't need to do anything. But I – wanted to let you know.

(Silence.)

ARNOLD. *(Finally.)* This is – great.

(Pause.)

JERRY. What?

ARNOLD. This is great, my *god*. What a relief.

(ARNOLD *takes a deep breath.)*

JERRY. Uh – yeah, she went peacefully –

ARNOLD. I mean it's done! She's gone! God, feels like a thousand pounds has just been lifted off my back or something –

JERRY. Okay –

ARNOLD. God, maybe this is – like, maybe this is exactly what I've been needing! I just needed to know I'm fucking *free*, I don't need to spend any more time thinking about her. Because it's done!

(Short pause.)

How do you feel?

(Pause.)

JERRY. You know, I've been taking care of her for almost a year now –

ARNOLD. Yeah, and now you're free!

JERRY. I guess?

ARNOLD. Now you get to have your life back!

JERRY. She was our mom, Arnie.

ARNOLD. Oh c'mon, you know how awful she was, we *both* know –

JERRY. But she was still our *mom* –

ARNOLD. And I mean, this means the two of us, *we* probably don't ever have to talk again! Right?! Like we can both just – walk away. We don't share anything anymore, we can just – walk away. For good.

(Pause.)

JERRY. I really think you should give Bram a call –

ARNOLD. No, you're not getting it – this means that both of us are finally *done*. You can do whatever you want! You always talked about how much you loved Arizona, you could move to Arizona! You never have to set foot in Grangeville ever again!

JERRY. I don't wanna leave Grangeville –

ARNOLD. WHY?! Dear god, Jerry, don't you see what a fucking *blessing* this is?! Both of us, we don't need to spend any more time thinking about those people –

JERRY. Who?

ARNOLD. *(Losing himself.)* EVERYONE! You, me, Mom, my dad, your dad, it's all fucking *done*! All these weeks I've been sitting around here, wondering if I should just buy a plane ticket to go back to Idaho just so I could, you know, fucking *say it* to Mom, to finally say *everything* I've been holding onto for decades, even if she couldn't actually understand me, just finally say *everything* to her, and now I don't have to think about that! I don't have to be that guy anymore, because it's done! SHE'S GONE! AND I WON'T EVER GET THE CHANCE TO SAY THOSE THINGS TO HER, I DON'T *NEED* TO SAY THOSE THINGS TO HER, IT'S FUCKING OVER, IT'S DONE, I –

> (**JERRY** *suddenly reaches out, grabbing* **ARNOLD**'s *arm.* **ARNOLD** *stops. They look at each other.)*

> (*Then, for the first time, a set is revealed: a life-sized diorama of the kitchen in the trailer where they grew up.)*

> (*There are half-packed boxes everywhere, stains on the carpet and ceilings, the endless detritus of decades of both children and adults living in a cramped space.)*

> (*The two* **MEN** *regard the trailer for a moment, then* **JERRY** *climbs inside. He stands at the kitchen table, looking at* **ARNOLD**.*)*

> (**ARNOLD** *waits a moment, then climbs into the diorama, joining* **JERRY**.*)*

> (*After a moment, they start sorting and packing: trash, donate, sell. Most of it is trash.* **JERRY** *sorts through old boxes;* **ARNOLD** *works on cleaning the kitchen.)*

> (**JERRY** *opens a box, looks inside. He pulls out a wad of old coupons.)*

JERRY. You gotta be shittin' me!

(**ARNOLD** *looks at him.*)

JERRY. Mom was a *coupon lady*?

(*Pause.* **JERRY** *looks through the coupons.*)

Ten bucks off an artificial Christmas tree? Do you remember us *ever* having a Christmas tree?

(**JERRY** *puts the coupons in the trash. He moves to a different box.*)

Think this is your old stuff. You wanna keep any of it?

ARNOLD. Uh – no, you can just toss it.

(**ARNOLD** *looks at him.* **JERRY** *takes out a well-worn stuffed dog from decades before.*)

JERRY. You sure you don't wanna keep Dog Dog?

(*Pause.* **ARNOLD** *looks at it for a moment, then looks away.*)

ARNOLD. Nah. Just toss him.

(**JERRY** *pauses for a moment, then puts the stuffed dog to the side in case* **ARNOLD** *changes his mind.*)

(**ARNOLD** *opens a kitchen cupboard, looking inside. He then reaches inside, pulling out a small statue of a thin man, vaguely reminiscent of a Giacometti sculpture.*)

(**ARNOLD** *puts the sculpture on the kitchen table.* **JERRY** *sees, stops working. The two* **MEN** *regard the sculpture for a moment.*)

JERRY. So whaddaya think?

(*Pause.* **ARNOLD** *looks at him.*)

ARNOLD. For fuck's sake, Jerry, no. This is not a real Giacometti.

(Short pause.)

JERRY. Yeah but are you *sure*?

ARNOLD. Yes! I am absolutely certain that Mom did not buy an original sculpture by Alberto Giacometti in a pawnshop in Burley.

*(Pause. **ARNOLD** goes back to the boxes. **JERRY** continues looking at the sculpture.)*

JERRY. Huh. Well, that's too bad then.

(Short pause.)

ARNOLD. How the hell did she even know who Giacometti was?

JERRY. Oh she had all those art books, you know.

(Short pause.)

ARNOLD. Art books?

JERRY. Yeah, you didn't know that? Last few years she was getting interested in that stuff, whattayacallit, art history. It was like her hobby. She even did some online course on the library computer.

*(Pause. **ARNOLD** thinks for a moment, looking at **JERRY**.)*

ARNOLD. Why?

*(**JERRY** looks at him. He shrugs.)*

JERRY. Dunno. She just liked it.

*(Pause. **ARNOLD** goes back to the boxes.)*

If I knew you were gonna come I would've held off on the funeral for a few days. I'm sorry you missed it.

(Short pause.)

JERRY. Only a handful of people showed up. Couple people I didn't even recognize. Pastor Ken, he gave the eulogy, it was fine I guess. But he hadn't talked to her in damn near ten years, he went on and on about how Mom would volunteer at the food bank? And I'm sitting there thinkin', he *definitely* has her mixed up with someone else.

(**JERRY** *pulls a deck of Uno cards out of a box.**)

Remember these?

(**ARNOLD** *looks, recognizing them.*)

We must have played this a million times.

ARNOLD. You were so obsessed with playing fucking Uno.

(Pause.)

JERRY. Me?

ARNOLD. Yeah, you'd get me to play this with you like every night –

JERRY. Buddy – you were the one who got *me* to play with you. You were ten years younger than me, don't you think I had better things to do?

*(Pause. **ARNOLD** thinks, looking away.)*

(**JERRY** *puts the cards down; they resume sorting.*)

I met with a real estate lady yesterday, she took a look around. She felt like with the condition it's in, we're not gonna be able to sell it. Gave me the number for some place that'll haul it off to the dump for us.

---

* A license to produce *Grangeville* does not include a license to publicly display any branded logos or trademarked images. Licensees must acquire rights for any logos and/or images or create their own.

ARNOLD. Oh.

    (Pause.)

(Looking around.) Yeah, I guess – I guess that makes sense.

    (Pause.)

Where are you gonna go?

    (Short pause.)

JERRY. I'll figure it out.

    (Short pause.)

How long are you gonna be in town?

ARNOLD. I – didn't book my return flight yet. Just didn't know how long I'd be.

JERRY. Does – Bram know you're here?

    *(Short pause. **ARNOLD** looks away.)*

ARNOLD. Uh...

JERRY. You didn't –?

ARNOLD. It's okay, just –.

    *(**ARNOLD** continues to work. **JERRY** looks at him for a moment, then goes back to sorting.)*

    (After a few moments:)

ARNOLD. The Dairy Queen closed.

    *(Short pause. **JERRY** stops, looking at him.)*

JERRY. Oh, yeah it –. Long time ago. Six, seven years ago? Has it really been that long since you –...?

ARNOLD. I guess so. Last time I was here, Tom was like four or five.

JERRY. Jeez, I guess you're right.

(*Pause.*)

They ask about you, now and then. Lauren and Tom.

ARNOLD. I still send birthday presents.

JERRY. That's why they ask about you.

ARNOLD. What do you tell them?

JERRY. That you – wanted to make your own life. Apart from us.

ARNOLD. That's it?

JERRY. What else am I supposed to tell them?

(*Pause.*)

ARNOLD. Do they know I'm married to a guy?

JERRY. Yeah, of course –

ARNOLD. Just wasn't sure if that was some dirty secret still, / or –

JERRY. Tom came out last year.

(**ARNOLD** *stops, looking at him. Pause.*)

It was a little tricky for him at first, but he's finding his way.

ARNOLD. He's –?

JERRY. Yeah. There's a couple other kids at the school who are gay, so he has his people. Or maybe they're not gay, they're – something else.

(*Pause.*)

It's not perfect around here, but it's – better. Better than what you went through.

(*Pause.*)

ARNOLD. And he's – okay? He's doing okay?

JERRY. I think so. Maybe you could ask him yourself?

(*Pause.* **ARNOLD** *looks away, becoming emotional.*)

ARNOLD. Yeah, maybe.

(*Short pause.*)

You know, I'm –. I'm pretty jet-lagged, I think I just need to go back to the hotel for a nap, I'll call you later –

JERRY. What do you need from me, Arnie?

(*Short pause.*)

ARNOLD. I don't – need anything from you –

JERRY. There's no way I can erase everything, I know / that –

ARNOLD. Okay / we're not doing this right now –

JERRY. And I'm not / asking for forgiveness –

ARNOLD. Just stop it. *Stop.*

JERRY. Do you wanna hit me?

(*Pause.*)

ARNOLD. *No* I don't / want to –

JERRY. Seriously, hit me. Right in the face, as hard as you can!

ARNOLD. Stop it!

(**JERRY** *goes to him.*)

JERRY. I know that won't solve it, but it's something! Just hit me as hard as you can, for all the shit I put you through, all this family put you through, all this *town* put you through –

ARNOLD. Shut the *fuck up*!

> (**ARNOLD** *pushes* **JERRY** *away. Short pause.* **JERRY** *looks at him.*)

JERRY. Okay.

> (**JERRY** *moves back toward* **ARNOLD.** **ARNOLD** *shoves him away again.*)

ARNOLD. Fucking *stop*!

> (**JERRY** *moves back toward* **ARNOLD;** **ARNOLD** *shoves him again.* **JERRY** *keeps provoking* **ARNOLD** *until they are in a full-on sibling wrestling match. It's awkward and pathetic, and lasts for too long.*)

> (*Finally,* **ARNOLD** *successfully shoves* **JERRY** *into the kitchen table. The sculpture gets knocked onto the floor; it shatters.*)

JERRY. You broke the Giacometti!

ARNOLD. IT'S NOT A FUCKING GIACOMETTI!

> (*Finally,* **ARNOLD** *pushes* **JERRY** *to the floor and gets him in a headlock.*)

JERRY. Okay, you win! I can't breathe!

ARNOLD. You are so *fucking selfish*, you know that?! What the *fuck* were you thinking trying to kill yourself?!

JERRY. What?!

ARNOLD. Do you know what that would have done to your fucking *kids*?! *You pathetic piece of shit!*

> (**ARNOLD** *tightens his grip.*)

JERRY. *...Please...*

*(Finally, **ARNOLD** releases him. **JERRY** falls to the ground. **JERRY** catches his breath as **ARNOLD** stands over him. Pause.)*

*(**JERRY** takes a few more breaths. **ARNOLD** sits down at the kitchen table. Silence.)*

How did you...?

(Short pause.)

ARNOLD. Mom left me a voicemail. After you did it. Or, tried to do it, whatever.

(Pause.)

ARNOLD. And I – never responded.

(Short pause.)

JERRY. Oh.

(Pause.)

I didn't –. I wasn't actually gonna go through with it, / I –

ARNOLD. Well your son found your fucking suicide note.

JERRY. It was just –. It was a dark time, Stacey was breaking up with me, Mom was sick... I walked up to the Lions Club Park with a gun but I ended up just coming right back down. I never would have gone through with it. But Tom had already found the note I left for Stacey, and –. It was a mess.

(Pause.)

You weren't supposed to know about that.

ARNOLD. Well I fucking know.

(Pause.)

I should have called.

JERRY. No, you –

ARNOLD. I *should have called.* I just – didn't know what to say.

>   (**ARNOLD** *takes a long breath. He looks at* **JERRY.**)

I don't know what the hell I'm doing, Jerry.

>   (*Pause.*)

JERRY. Arnie – you *really* should call Bram.

ARNOLD. Yeah...

JERRY. And buy your return ticket.

>   (*Short pause.*)

You need to go back home.

>   (**ARNOLD** *looks at him.*)

>   (*Pause.* **ARNOLD** *looks at* **JERRY** *for a moment, then grabs the deck of Uno cards.*)

>   (**ARNOLD** *sits down on the floor and deals each of them seven cards.*)

>   (**JERRY** *pauses a moment, then goes to* **ARNOLD**, *getting down onto the ground as well.*)

Oof, my knees.

>   (**JERRY** *sits.*)

You remember how to play?

ARNOLD. Think so.

>   (**ARNOLD** *plays a card.* **JERRY** *does as well.*)

>   (**ARNOLD** *plays another.* **JERRY** *draws a card.*)

Wait, with the – with the Skip card, you –

JERRY. I think you just skip me, so you can play again.

>*(**ARNOLD** plays two cards. **JERRY** plays a card.)*

Yellow.

ARNOLD. Crap.

>*(**ARNOLD** draws a card. **JERRY** plays a card.)*

JERRY. Skip.

>*(**JERRY** plays another card.)*

>*(**ARNOLD** plays another card.)*

ARNOLD. Red.

>*(**JERRY** plays a card.)*

>*(**ARNOLD** plays another card. **JERRY** plays another.)*

>*(**ARNOLD** draws a card. **JERRY** plays a card. He's down to one.)*

JERRY. Uno.

>*(**ARNOLD** plays a card.)*

>*(**JERRY** looks at the last card in his hand. Pause.)*

ARNOLD. You gonna win?

>*(**JERRY** looks at him for a moment, then draws a card.)*

JERRY. Your turn.

>*(**ARNOLD** looks at him for a moment, then plays a card. He's down to one.)*

ARNOLD. Uno.

JERRY. Still can't go.

ARNOLD. Really?

(**JERRY** *shrugs.*)

JERRY. Bad luck.

(**JERRY** *draws another card.* **ARNOLD** *looks at the last remaining card in his hand.*)

(*Then,* **ARNOLD** *starts to fight a massive wave of tears. He takes a few deep breaths, struggling to maintain himself, months of tension washing out of him.*)

(*Finally, he lays down the card, winning the game. Pause.*)

There you go.

(**ARNOLD** *looks up at* **JERRY.**)

End of Play

www.ingramcontent.com/pod-product-compliance
Lightning Source LLC
Chambersburg PA
CBHW070646120726
47909CB00004B/1598